KT-430-411

Stewart, Judy, *1948–*
Family in Sudan.
1. Sudan – Social life and customs –
Juvenile literature
I. Title II. Matthews, Jenny
962.4'04 DT154.9

ISBN 0–7136–2921–5

A & C Black (Publishers) Limited
35 Bedford Row, London WC1R 4JH

Acknowledgements
The map is by Tony Garrett

Filmset by August Filmsetting, Haydock, St Helens
Printed in Hong Kong by Dai Nippon Printing Co. Ltd

Family in Sudan

Judy Stewart

Photographs by Jenny Matthews

A & C Black · London

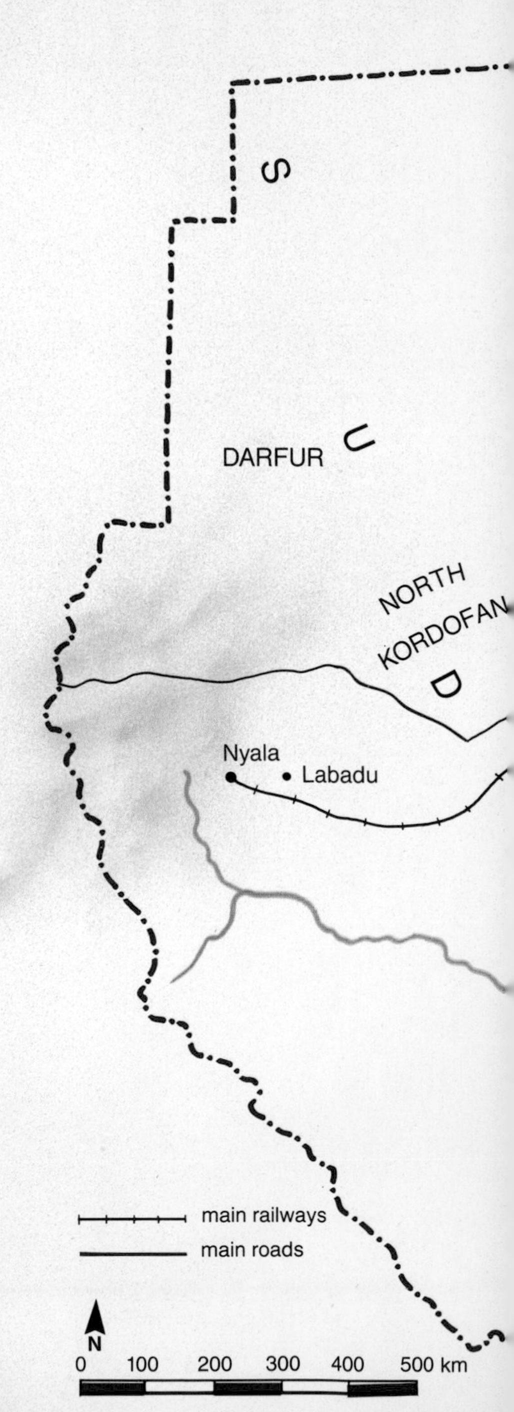

My name is Dawalbeit and I'm ten years old. My name means 'Light of the House'. I live in a village called Labadu, in the west of Sudan.

Sudan is the biggest country in Africa. My family's quite big too. Here we are, putting on our biggest smiles for the photograph. That's me – in the front, second from the left. And there's Grandad and two of my grannies. There's Mum and Dad and Dad's other wife, Medina.

We are Muslims and in our religion a man can have up to four wives. But he must treat them all the same. So if Dad buys Mum a new dress, he buys one for Medina too.

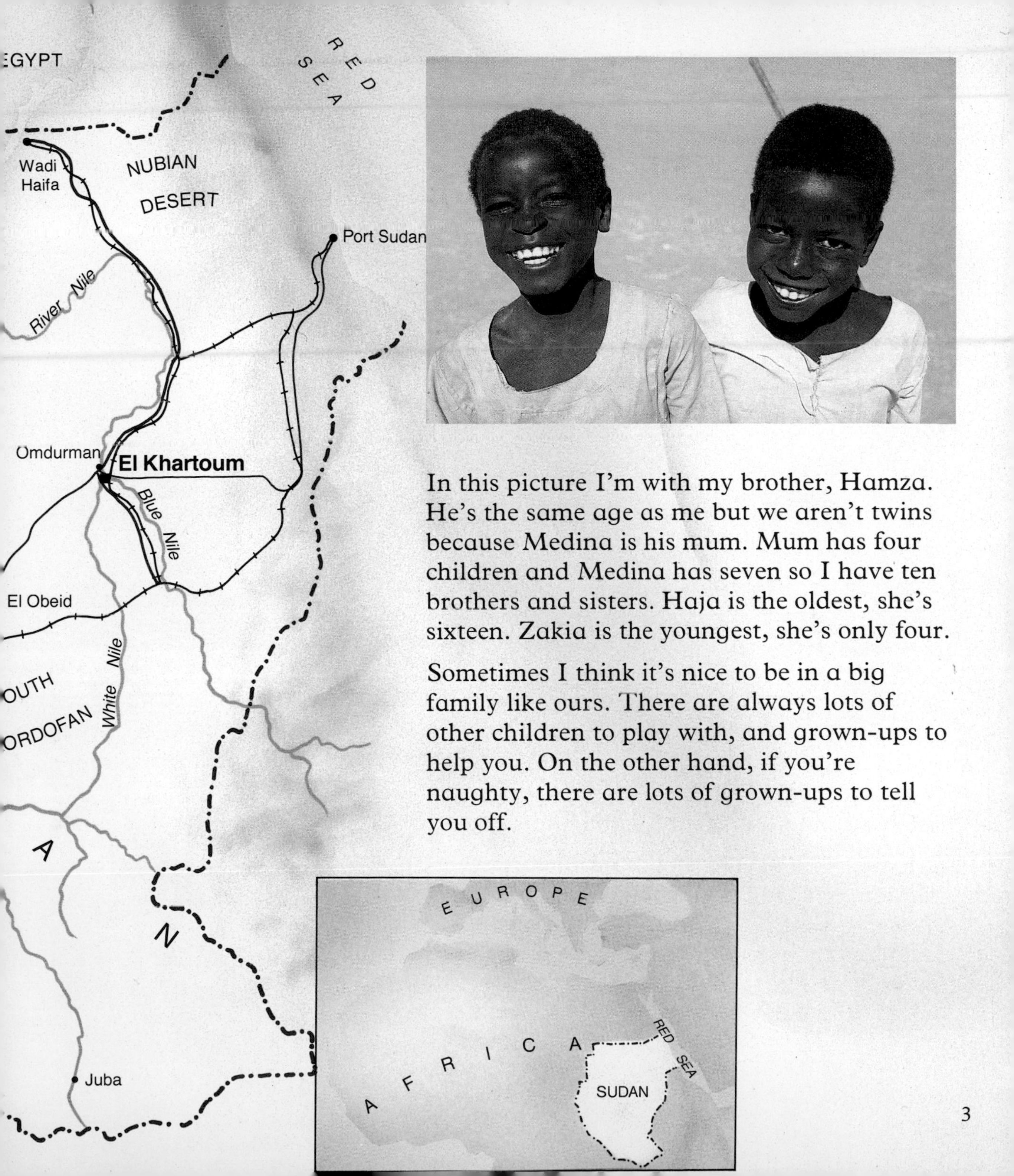

In this picture I'm with my brother, Hamza. He's the same age as me but we aren't twins because Medina is his mum. Mum has four children and Medina has seven so I have ten brothers and sisters. Haja is the oldest, she's sixteen. Zakia is the youngest, she's only four.

Sometimes I think it's nice to be in a big family like ours. There are always lots of other children to play with, and grown-ups to help you. On the other hand, if you're naughty, there are lots of grown-ups to tell you off.

My family lives inside a compound which is surrounded by a high fence. Inside the compound there are seven huts made out of millet stalks. The huts are divided amongst my family. I share one with Grandad, because I'm the oldest boy.

Most mornings, the first thing I hear is the thumping sound of someone pounding millet into flour. We eat far more millet than any other food, and have it at least twice a day. I get up at six o'clock and have a glass of sweet milky tea. We all start work early because it gets so hot later on.

Every day, from June until November, some of the family go out to our fields. It takes one and a half hours to walk there and we have to set off as early as possible while it's still cool. There isn't any water nearby, so we take some with us.

We grow millet in the fields because it can stand very dry weather. We also grow water-melons to give water to our animals and because we sell the seeds to make oil. I use a mallet to break open the water-melon and get to the seeds.

We're lucky to have some land along the river bed where we can grow vegetables. Dad says it's good to have different kinds of crops so that if some don't grow, others will.

We get back home before ten o'clock, so that we're in time for breakfast. On the way home from the fields we always look for firewood, because there aren't many trees near the village.

Mum, Zubida and Neimat carry the wood home on their heads. Mum says it's the best way to carry a heavy load, but she sometimes gets a headache if she has to walk a long way.

Everything stops for breakfast. We usually have asida, which is a stiff porridge made of millet flour and water. We take it in turns to help cook. You eat asida with sauce made out of vegetables and dried meat.

A big family like mine needs a lot of water for cooking, drinking and washing. Mum and my older sisters make several trips to the village well every day. They take buckets and pottery jars – the jars are heavy but they keep the water cool.

Neimat's very good at balancing on the edge of the well while she pulls up the bucket. The water is a long way down. There's always a big group of people waiting at the well to throw down their buckets, so it's a good place to chat and catch up on all the news.

While Mum is working, she and Medina and my grannies like to sit together in the shade. Then they can chat and drink tea while they do different jobs.

Medina weaves tabacs, which are covers made out of raffia. You put them over food to keep away flies and dust. It's so hot and dry in Labadu that there's always a lot of dust.

You can tell where a tabac was made because different villages make them in different patterns and colours. Medina's one of the best tabac weavers in my village. My sisters all want to learn from her.

Medina spends some time plaiting Neimat's hair. She uses a long pin to separate the hair into thin strands, then she makes lots of little plaits all over Neimat's head. It takes a long time to do, but Medina says it's worth it because when she's finished Neimat looks so neat and nice.

While it's being done, Neimat passes the time watching Granny make peanut butter, and listening to everyone talking.

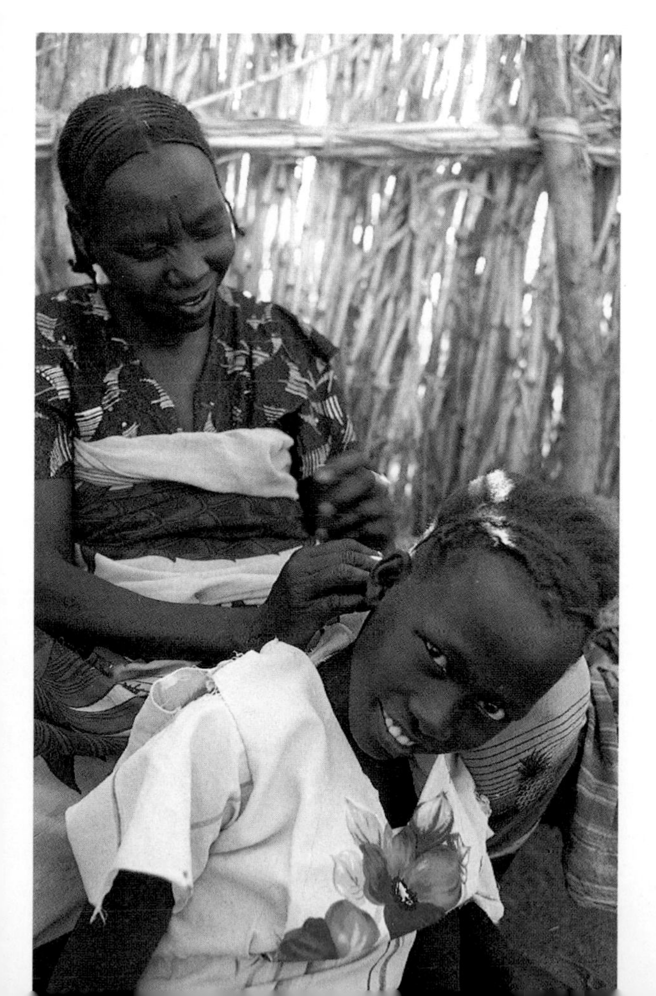

Granny uses peanut butter in quite a lot of sauces. Hamza and I have to shell the peanuts, then Granny roasts them and grinds them into a paste. She keeps some for cooking and sells the rest in the market. I love peanut butter. If I could, I'd just go on eating it forever.

I go to school in Labadu, with five of my brothers and sisters. School starts at nine o'clock and finishes at half past one, with a break for breakfast at ten o'clock. We learn Arabic, maths, religion and science.

Here we're learning verses from the Koran, our Holy Book. Our teacher writes the first bit on the blackboard and asks someone to stand up and say the whole verse. If we know the answer, we shout, 'Sir! Sir!' That's an English word – I don't know why we say it, except that a long time ago Sudan was ruled by England and Egypt, and being able to speak English was quite important then.

My sister, Haja, is learning English at her school in Nyala. Sometimes she tries to teach us a few words. It isn't anything like Arabic, though.

My dad knows the Koran off by heart. He prays five times every day. First he takes out his prayer mat and washes his feet. He begins his prayers by saying 'God is great. There is no God but God, and Mohammed is his prophet.'

We believe that everything that happens to us is because of God. When we talk about something in the future, we always say 'Inshallah' which means 'If God wants this to happen'. When I say goodbye to my school friends, I say 'See you tomorrow, Inshallah'.

Friday is our holy day, and Dad goes off to the mosque with the other men. Mum prays at home with Medina and my grannies. Afterwards Dad meets his friends at the tea shop to talk about the price of grain.

On Friday night and early Saturday morning, lorries arrive in Labadu, loaded with things to sell. Saturday is market day, and people come from miles around, on the lorries, by camel or donkey, or on foot. The rest of the week the market place is empty, then suddenly it's full of stalls selling food, clothes, beds, buckets – all kinds of things.

It's a really busy day for our family: Zubida sells vegetables, Medina sells peanut butter and herbs, Haja's helping out on an onion stall, Mum's running a tea stall, and Grandad's selling goatskins with his friends.

During the week, Dad has a shop, but on Saturdays he shuts it and has a stall in the market. I take it in turns with Neimat to help on the stall. We sell things like soap, tea, salt and dried vegetables. It's hard work counting and weighing things, and working out the change – I'm getting really good at doing sums in my head.

When I get the chance, I go over to the shop nearby which sells fancy things from town. The man in the shop plays music all day on his cassette recorder. Most of the time he plays Sudanese music, but he likes American singers too. I like listening to Michael Jackson and Bob Marley.

It's great having so many brothers and sisters to play with. When I'm not at school or helping Dad, I love playing football. I support the Nyala team. They wear red shorts, and they're very good players. If I had red shorts I'd be a faster runner – my gellabia gets in the way a bit.

Another game I like playing is called 'seiga'. For a board, we make a square out of holes in the sand, and play with stones or bottle tops. It's a bit complicated to explain the rules, but to win you have to capture most of the other player's stones. My brother Hamza hates losing so there's always a fuss if I beat him.

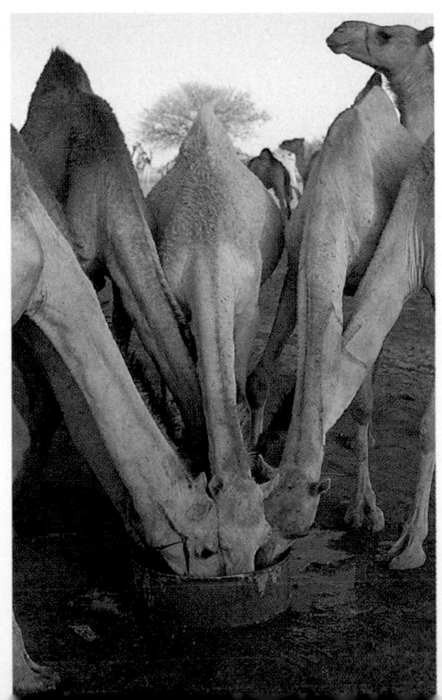

Sometimes in the school holidays we go and visit our cousins in the next village. Last week a group of people passed by on their way to a wedding in the village. They stopped near our compound to give their camels some water. They said it took them two days journey by camel from their home.

The quickest way to travel round here is by lorry. I know the names of all the lorries that come to Labadu – there's Nissan, and Fiat and Austin, as well as the Land Rovers.

Sometimes I go to Nyala with Dad to buy things for our shop. The roads aren't very good and it's a slow, bumpy, dusty journey. In the rainy season it takes even longer because the lorries get stuck in the mud.

In Nyala we can take the bus. It's a much busier town than Labadu – there's an enormous market where we can buy lots of things we can't get at home.

Outside Nyala there's a big animal market. Most of the animals are sold as food for people in Khartoum, the capital city, or abroad. The lorries that take the animals to Khartoum pass by Labadu on the way east. Dad says it can take them ten days to get there.

There aren't enough jobs for everyone round here so lots of people go east to find work. My uncle Amin went to Khartoum three years ago. He's come back twice since then, bringing money for my grandparents and presents and lots of stories for us.

Uncle Amin says that Khartoum is huge and busy. The streets are full of traffic, there are big shops and hotels and a big football stadium with floodlights.

We can't ever be sure if there'll be enough rain here, or if it will fall at the right time to make our crops grow. It can be difficult growing enough grain to eat.

Everybody tries to be prepared just in case we have a bad year. My family stores as much grain as it can. When the rains are good, we grow enough millet to last us two or three years. In the picture, Granny is throwing the millet in the air so that the grain falls back into her basket and the rubbish blows away.

Some people in the village store their grain in big jars. We keep ours in a hole in the ground. It's safe there from mice and insects.

Dad thinks it's important to have different kinds of animals because some are tougher than others. Cows are worth a lot, but they suffer most when it doesn't rain. Goats are tougher, but not worth as much. Camels can go for days with no water and they can carry heavy loads, but they cost a lot.

Most of the time our animals are kept close to the village, but if there isn't much rain, they have to be taken quite a long way away to find food.

It's easier for some of our friends because they are nomads. In the dry season, they go a long way south with the animals, and we don't see them again until the rainy season.

In the dry season, we have to watch out for a terrible wind called the haboob. When it blows, the sky goes red with all the dust and soil. It gets in your eyes and ears, and when it's gone by, everything is covered in thick dust.

The big problem with the haboob is that it carries the good soil away and makes it difficult to grow things. This hut belonged to my aunt. Last year when she was away, the haboob covered her hut with sand. Some of my friends say it's even worse in the north, especially where the animals have eaten all the grass. Their families had to move down here because they couldn't live in their village any more.

The last few years, we've had much less rain than normal, and last year it didn't rain at all. After our hard work planting, nothing grew. Soon, we'd used up all our millet stores. In the market, millet got very expensive because there wasn't enough and everybody wanted some. At the same time, Dad couldn't get much money for our animals because they were so thin.

All my auntie's animals were sold or died. She went to Nyala to find work, because she didn't have any food left. It was difficult to manage. We used to have 30 cows, 70 sheep, 40 goats and three donkeys. All of our cows, sheep and donkeys died, and we sold or ate most of the goats. All we have left are twelve goats and a new horse we've just bought.

Mum tried to make our millet go further by mixing it with wild plants. She used to send us out to get them. We used to spend a long time looking – there are so many different kinds. Some are easy to find because we pick them every year to put in our sauces. They grow in the dried-up river bed. Others are more difficult, but Neimat knows a lot about which ones are all right to pick.

The plant we picked most is called mukheit. Mum would dry it in the sun, and soak it for a long time. Then she would have to boil it three times before making it into soup. It tasted horrible and once I had a bad stomach ache afterwards. We couldn't have any milk either, because the goats were too thin to give any.

After a while we were having two small meals instead of three every day. We ate more and more wild plants and less and less millet. Haja went to stay with Mum's brother in Nyala. They sent us a small sack of millet.

My little brothers and sisters didn't understand what the matter was, and they would ask for more dinner. All the grown-ups looked tired and worried.

One day in April, a lorry came to the village with lots of sacks of sorghum, sent from abroad. Everyone crowded round, but there wasn't much for each family – about half a pound of grain to last each person a month. Sorghum doesn't taste as good as millet, but it's much better than mukheit.

In June the rains came at last, and most of the people who had left the village came back to plant their crops. My auntie came back too – we were so pleased to see her.

Auntie told us about all the people who had tried to find food and work in the town. It was very difficult: lots of them were ill and some died.

The government set up a camp outside Nyala, and sent food and medicine to it, but there wasn't enough to go round. I won't forget that year – it was a terrible time for all of us.

When the rains came we had hope, but still no food until we could harvest our crops in November. Lots of the lorries bringing food from abroad couldn't get to us until after the rainy season. Then, when the harvest came, we didn't need the food from abroad.

When we brought in our millet harvest, we were really happy. There was enough to eat, and some to store. Everybody began to look fatter and healthier again. God has brought us rain, and 'Inshallah' next year the rains will come again.